G000166154

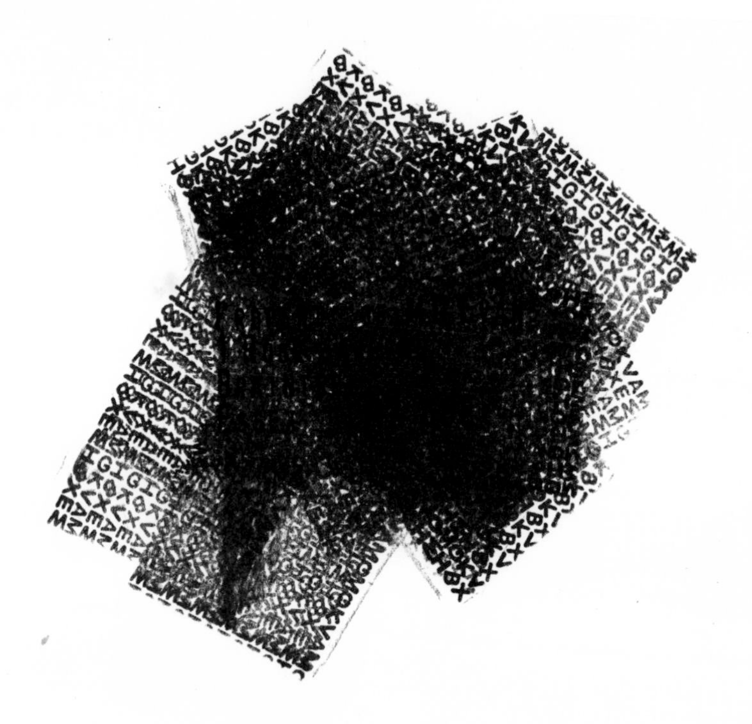

# Goblin Party

DOUGLAS HILL

ILLUSTRATED BY
PAUL DEMEYER

LONDON
VICTOR GOLLANCZ LTD
1988

Colin and his parents were on a camping holiday in the mountains, and Colin was having a fine time. He enjoyed hiking through the woods in the hollows and vales. Even more, he enjoyed scrambling up rocky paths to the higher slopes, like a real mountain-climber. And it was fun to eat meals cooked on a little camp-stove and to sleep in his sleeping bag in a tent.

He also enjoyed the stories that his father told about the mountains — especially the ones about the demons and witches and other weird creatures that were supposed to live there in the olden days.

"There are some stories," Colin's father said one day, "about people who disappeared in these mountains and were never seen again. One story . . ."

But Colin's mother stopped him. "That's enough of that," she said firmly. "He's only nine — you'll give him nightmares with your stories."

Colin's father winked at Colin, and started talking about all the plants around them instead of scary stories. But Colin didn't mind. He had found that he could make up his own stories, quite spooky enough. He only had to look around — at the dark hollows with strange rustlings in the brush, or the large rocks and boulders looming like giants, or the twisted trees reaching out with branches like long claws.

But in the middle of the next night, when Colin came suddenly wide awake, it seemed that his mother had been right about stories giving him bad dreams.

The tent should have been totally dark, for there were no lights anywhere. Yet Colin found that he could see perfectly well. The trouble was, he wished that he couldn't. For something very ugly was standing beside his sleeping bag.

The creature was no taller than Colin, but it would have been frightening whatever its size. Its skin was greenish-yellow, all wrinkled and warty, and it wore a ragged shirt and trousers that seemed to be made of mouldy bark. It had a tuft of tangled black hair on its pointed head and also on the tip of each pointed ear. Its nose looked like a lumpy green potato, and its eyes were huge, yellow and slanted. Its thick-lipped mouth was full of sharp teeth and there were long claws on its fingers and toes.

Colin was nearly sick with fright. Even inside his warm sleeping bag he began shivering from head to toe as he stared at the creature. He tried to call out to his parents, but his throat was so tight with terror that he could not make a sound.

The green-skinned monster smiled, showing more of its teeth. "No use yellin' out, boy," it said in a sharp, scratchy voice. "Yer folks'll stay sound asleep. Goblin magic is seein' to that."

When Colin heard the words "goblin magic", he was suddenly less afraid. It's a *dream*, he told himself. Just like mum said.

He sat up slowly, wide-eyed but no longer shivering. The goblin nodded with what seemed to be approval.

"Gettin' over yer scare?" it said. "Good fer you. Shouldn't go to a goblin party scared out of yer wits."

Colin blinked with surprise, then gasped. As the goblin waved one grimy green hand, something seemed to lift Colin up out of the sleeping bag.

"Name's Rankle, by the way," the goblin was saying with a leer. "Don't need to know *yer* name. Reckon you might have 'nother one 'fore this night's done."

With that he rose from the ground and floated out through the door of the tent, with Colin drifting after him. Colin might have been puzzled about what the goblin had said, about his name — but just then he was more concerned with what was happening to him. They were gathering speed, flying up towards the mountain peaks that rose like vast black shadows against the night sky.

Gathering a little courage, Colin found his voice. "Where . . . where are we going?" he called.

The goblin, Rankle, turned and grinned. "Told you — to a goblin party. Y'know what they say — the more the scarier. And yer a guest of honour."

They soared up, high over the mountain peaks, and Colin realised that he didn't feel cold, even though he was barefoot and in his pyjamas. More goblin magic, he told himself, which was probably also why he could see in the dark. It's a good nightmare, he thought — it's taking care of everything. As they flew on, he was half-hoping that he wouldn't wake up before he saw what a goblin party was like.

Then they began to drift down, as softly as falling leaves. Below them Colin could see a mountain-top that was almost flat, like a wide basin. On it grew some coarse grass, with a half-dead tree at one side. At the other side a huge bonfire was blazing, and around the fire some large rocks were scattered, flat-topped like crude tables. They were piled high with mounds of stuff that perhaps was food, and crowded with many bottles and flagons.

Around those tables, jostling and pointing as they stared up at Colin, were the guests at the goblin party.

Colin was staring too, as his feet touched the damp ground beside the half-dead tree. Once again he was shaking, and his voice seemed to have stopped working. Then Rankle, the goblin, waved a hand, and a long jet-black cord appeared from nowhere. One end tied itself to the tree while the other end wrapped around Colin's waist, like a belt, feeling icy cold.

"Don't want you wanderin' off," Rankle said, with his nasty grin. "Might come to some harm."

All the crowd began to laugh — cackling, howling, whooping, grunting, hooting, shrieking and worse. It was such a wave of noise that it nearly knocked Colin over. He shrank away, trying to get behind the tree. But Rankle grabbed his arm and dragged him forward.

"Don't hang back, boy," he said. "You got to meet these folks, start gettin' to know 'em."

As the crowd turned back to the food and drink, Rankle began to tell Colin about the monsters. First he pointed out the large number of green-skinned goblins. "You can tell goblins," Rankle said. "All good-lookin' folks, like me. All *family*."

Then Rankle pointed to other creatures. They looked something like goblins, but they were different sizes and colours — greyish-white, muddy purple, rusty brown — and some had flatter heads or bigger ears.

"All them's sort of *cousins* of the goblins," Rankle said. "Some're called bogans, some're pookas. The stooped-over ones with the teeth are spriggans."

Colin shuddered and closed his eyes. But

he opened them at once when Rankle squeezed his arm painfully.

"Pay 'tention now," the goblin snarled. "See the big fellers back in the shadow, with the round heads an' huge boots, lookin' like they're made of rusted metal? Trolls, they are. An' there's some ogres too, not quite so big, lookin' more like folks. An' if you look close you can see the little ones, all gnarled an' hunched with long arms. They're gnomes."

Colin shuddered again. "I want to wake up now," he whispered.

Rankle ignored him. "Those folks stay back 'cause they don't like the light much," he went on. "Not like the imps — see the little fellers round the fire, all covered in hair, with goat's hooves? An' if you look close you can spot a few fellers with big ears, all in green — see, there! Leprechauns, they are, from a land a long way away."

He went on, pointing to more of the hideous figures. Colin flinched away from the sight of several huge black dogs with blood-red mouths and enormous fiery eyes. Bogles, or grims, Rankle called them. Nearby were a few shapeless, misty things that shone with a pale eerie light. Rankle said they were Will-o'-the-wisps, who led people into the depths of fens and marshes, never to be seen again. And at one side were some four-footed creatures called kelpies, which might have been ordinary

ponies — except that they were glistening wet, with fierce crimson eyes and cruel, sharp-pointed teeth.

There were others, too, whose names were too strange for Colin to understand or remember. By then he was dizzy with fear and disgust, from being so close to so much horror out of ancient tales and legends. But as he sagged against the tree, Rankle chortled.

"Count yerself lucky, boy. Yer gettin' to

see the magic folk. Not the other sort, o' course — yer fairies an' elves an' pixies an' the like. We got no dealin's with *them*. This party's just for the *bad* ones. So you watch an' listen, boy, an' learn, while I get somethin' to eat an' say hello to folks."

Rankle moved away to join the others. For a while the crowd of monsters left Colin alone. They seemed more interested in jostling around the heaped tables, stuffing great handfuls of the disgusting-looking food into their mouths and taking huge gulps from the many bottles. It seemed that the food and drink were magical, too. There was never any less, no matter how the creatures gorged — just as the fire never burned down.

As he watched, Colin told himself over and over that it was all only a dream. It was strange that he hadn't wakened up yet, but it had to be a dream. There were *no such things*, he said to himself, as goblins and trolls and all the rest.

He straightened up, trying to ignore the icy cord around his waist, trying to look at the creatures without shivering. Then Rankle ambled back towards him, holding a small flagon in one hand and a lump of something pink and oozing in the other.

"Feelin' better?" the goblin asked. "That's the way. Got to start gettin' used to us sometime. Here — brought you somethin' to eat an' drink."

Colin took the flagon and the squelchy glob and stared at them, feeling sick. He knew that he could not possibly bring either of them near his mouth. The liquid in the flagon smelled like it had come from a drain, and the pink lump smelled — and looked — as if it had been going rotten for weeks.

Rankle was watching with a frown. "Ain't you goin' to eat it? It's good grub."

Colin knew he had to do something, for he had no wish to anger the goblin. Sensibly, he changed the subject.

"What did you mean," he asked, "about me having to . . . to start getting used to you?"

Rankle's wide grin showed an alarming number of teeth. "Wondered if you caught that. I was talkin' 'bout why you're here. But you'll find out all 'bout that, soon . . ."

He stopped. The entire throng had suddenly burst out into another wild explosion of screeching, bellowing and howling. Colin saw that all the monsters were looking upwards, and that the din was a greeting.

Down from the night sky, like some huge ungainly bird, flew a terrifying woman.

She was perched on an old-fashioned broom made of twigs tied to a long handle. Dark robes fluttering, weird white hair standing up like spikes, she swooped down to land by the fire.

Colin saw that she was not terribly old, despite her white hair, for she was not bent or stooped. But whatever her age, she was horrible. Her lips were scarlet, as were her long, curved fingernails. Her eyes glared yellow as flames from beneath her white eyebrows. And the skin of her face and hands was a lurid, electric blue.

It's a *dream*, Colin reminded himself sternly. He was standing alone again, for Rankle had hurried over to join the others, greeting the new arrival.

While the crowd of monsters was fully occupied with the fearsome woman, Colin carefully reached behind the tree and poured out the foul liquid from the flagon.

Then he stared at the handful of revolting food. If he just tossed it aside, he thought, Rankle or one of the other creatures might see it, and become angry. So instead he jammed the smelly glob into the pocket of his pyjama top, hoping no one would notice.

Meanwhile the tumult over by the fire had died down a little. The blue-faced woman was grinning at everyone, waving her broomstick, chattering noisily, shrieking with laughter. Then she turned towards Colin. As her glowing eyes stared at him, she licked her scarlet lips with a scarlet tongue.

"I see you have a guest," she hissed. "Someone introduce me!"

Rankle brought her over to where Colin was tied. "Boy," said the goblin, "this here's the Lady Vinegra, one of the most famous witches in the whole land. We're real lucky she's come to our party."

Colin stared up fearfully as the witch, Vinegra, reached out with a clawed forefinger and prodded him in the stomach.

"Healthy enough," she said, looking pleased. "Do we serve him up in morsels for everyone, or roast him later for just a few of us?"

Rankle looked upset. "We ain't goin' to *eat* him, Vinegra. That ain't why I went an' got him."

"It isn't?" The witch's smile turned into a scowl. "You're not playing that silly old game again, are you, Rankle?"

"That's why I got him," the goblin said stubbornly.

Vinegra sighed. "Oh, well. If you must. It seems such a waste. But he *is* yours, I suppose."

"Right," Rankle agreed. "Rules is rules. An' it'll be a laugh — you'll see."

"If you say so," the witch replied. She turned her scowl on to Colin, then wandered back to the crowd gathered around the laden tables.

Rankle stayed briefly, picking up Colin's flagon, which had magically become full again. "Want me to leave this, or you had enough?"

Colin, struggling to be brave, shook his head no. "I want to know what's *happening*. What were you saying, before? Why did you bring me here?"

"Yer here to be a guest of honour, like I said," Rankle told him with another toothy grin. "Don't worry 'bout it. Enjoy the party."

He drifted away, still grinning.

Colin sank back against the tree. He felt more and more sure that something very bad was going to happen to him, sooner or later. Also, he was feeling less and less sure that it was all a dream. It wasn't all muddled and crazy, as dreams usually are, and it was going on so long — past the time when he usually woke up from a dream.

By then it was far past the middle of the night, and the creatures were growing even more rowdy. Some weird music had begun playing — out of thin air — which Colin found painfully loud and harsh. But the creatures seemed to enjoy it. Some were singing along with it, sounding harsher than the music. A great many were dancing — leaping, hopping, spinning, clumping, round and round. Quite a few of the dancers grew so excited

that they floated up into the air and danced there, sometimes upside down. And all the while, other monsters went on eating, drinking, laughing, quarrelling, screeching, howling . . .

Through all their wild antics, the uproarious monsters did not leave Colin completely alone. Goblins danced past and leered at him with grins that seemed to promise new horrors to come. Trolls and gnomes bared their teeth at him, howling with laughter when he shrank back. Imps appeared from nowhere beside him, pinching him or pulling his hair, laughing shrilly before disappearing again.

Worst of all, more than once he saw the witch, Vinegra, staring hot-eyed at him, licking her lips.

Sometimes, though, Colin would have a few moments' peace — especially when the black dogs started a fight with some gnomes. All of them ended up in a wild tangle, snapping and growling and tumbling among the tables, while all the other creatures yelled encouragement. And when the dogs and gnomes wearily stopped their fight, another battle started up between some bogans and the imps. So the party went on, more and more riotous, as the hours drifted past.

Finally, Vinegra sprang on to her broomstick and rose several feet from the ground. With a gesture of one red-clawed hand, she brought a mighty blast of thunder — which rattled all the rocks on the mountain-top and stunned the party into silence.

"Listen to me!" she yelled. "It is now growing close to dawn, and the party's end!"

A groan swept through the throng, silenced at once by Vinegra's glare.

"But we still have our guest of honour!" she shouted. "And I still say that the boy should be prepared as a special delicacy, so that each of us can taste a bit of him!"

The crowd shrieked in evil agreement — until an even louder voice cut across the outcry.

*"You will NOT!"*

It was Rankle, looking furious. Around him, also looking angry and dangerous, were all the other green-skinned goblins, his "family". And around them, glowering, stood the others that were their "cousins" — the bogans and pookas and spriggans.

"This's a *goblin* party, Vinegra," Rankle said with a snarl. "Like I told you, *I* went an' got the boy. He's *mine*. An' you know what I'm goin' to do with him. You know it's the only way fer us to make more goblins."

"I'd say there's enough of you already," Vinegra muttered.

Rankle went on as if he had not heard. "So just ferget it. You ain't eatin' him. He belongs to the goblins — that's the Rules. You want to break the Rules? You want to go against all of us?"

For a moment Vinegra glared down at them, her yellow eyes blazing. Then the mass of goblins and their relatives took a menacing step forward — and the witch drew back.

"Oh, do what you like," she said crossly. "I've had enough of you and your party."

With a whistling howl like a winter wind, Vinegra's broomstick swept her high into the darkness and out of sight.

Then Rankle and the other goblin-creatures, followed by the rest of the monsters, turned and walked purposefully towards Colin.

"Now, boy," said the grinning Rankle, "here's yer big moment."

"Wh . . . what are you going to do to me?" Colin asked fearfully.

"Why, we're goin' to make you part of the family," Rankle told him. "We're goin' to turn you into a goblin."

Colin stared — so startled that he almost forgot to be terrified. "But you . . . you *can't*!" he burst out. "You wouldn't be *allowed*! It's . . . against the *law*!"

The entire crowd collapsed into hilarious laughter, more frighteningly noisy than Vinegra's clap of thunder. As the noise died down, Rankle shook his head with his mocking grin.

"Yer law don't touch us, boy," he said. "We do what we like. Always have. 'Cept fer our own Rules."

"Rules?" Colin asked shakily, remembering that Rankle had talked about rules when facing Vinegra.

"The Ghoulish Rules," Rankle said. "Only thing that tells us what we can do, or not. What tells us to be out of sight by daybreak — an' makes us stay away from silver an' iron an' garlic an' other stuff. Rules like that."

Colin just blinked at him, speechlessly.

"Rules say we can carry off human kids," Rankle went on. "An' keep 'em if we want. Like we aim to keep you, and make you into a goblin. But Rules say some things got to *happen* 'fore we can keep you."

Rankle leaned closer, his voice serious. "Rules say we got to give you a special *test.* Unnerstand? Rules say we can keep you only if you *fail* the test."

Colin felt something very faint, like hope, stirring within him.

"'Course you prob'ly will fail," Rankle said with satisfaction. "The test's a fearsome hard *riddle.* You get the answer wrong, you're a goblin with us ferever an' ever..."

The faint hope withered within Colin, as Rankle stepped closer to him.

"You ready, then?" the goblin asked. "Ready fer the riddle?" Without waiting for an answer, he glanced around at the others, grinning — then turned back to Colin and spoke the riddle.

"*Where was the hobgoblin,*" he asked, "*when the light went out?*"

For a long moment Colin stood absolutely still, as if frozen, his mind completely empty. He saw all the goblin-creatures snickering and nudging one another. But he couldn't speak, couldn't even think — because he couldn't believe what he had heard.

"Too hard fer you, ain't it?" Rankle said, clearly enjoying Colin's fear and his blank silence.

Colin opened his mouth, but no sound came out. That made the creatures laugh even harder, but he barely heard them. He was still in a daze, because he couldn't believe it.

Rankle had said that all he had to do was answer the riddle. Yet, as far as Colin could tell, it was simply a version of one of the oldest, easiest and silliest riddles in the world.

"Don't know, do you?" Rankle said, his nasty grin stretched to its widest. "C'mon — last chance. Where was the hobgoblin when the light went out?"

Colin took a deep breath, and found his voice. "Er . . . it's . . . I think . . ." He paused — then, in a rush, said the answer that he had known all along. "*In the dark*!"

Utter silence fell over the mountain-top. The smiles and snickers of the creatures disappeared like blown-out candle flames.

A murmur that was almost a groan swept through the throng, full of disappointment. Looking downcast and glum, the monsters shook their heads and shuffled and began to turn away.

Rankle was staring at Colin, totally thunderstruck. “Didn’t think you’d get it,” he said unhappily. “But yer just like all the rest, fer the last couple hundred years. Why do I always pick the *clever* kids?”

Colin almost got the giggles, from sheer relief. He also almost told Rankle that the riddle was foolishly easy. But he stopped himself. If the whole thing was *not* a dream, he thought, other children might be carried off by the goblins. And they too would need a nice easy riddle to answer.

One of the ogres turned back. “Could still eat him, maybe?” he said hopefully.

"Can't," Rankle said. "Rules is Rules."

At that moment there were gasps and cries from the midst of the throng. Some of the creatures were pointing to the east — where a faint smear of grey light in the sky showed that dawn was just about to break. In a sudden flurry of movement like a swirl of dead leaves, the creatures disappeared into nothingness, until all of them were gone.

Then the cord vanished from Colin's waist, and he was lifted into the air by Rankle's magic. At high speed they hurtled

over the mountain peaks, swooping breathlessly down towards the tent. A blink of an eye later, he found himself tucked back into his sleeping bag — amazed that his parents were still asleep, amazed that the whole terrifying adventure had ended so swiftly.

Rankle stood awkwardly beside him for a moment. "Well — 'bye," he said. "Sorry we couldn't keep you. But now you don't need to be scared no more. Rules say none of us can ever carry you off again, never."

With that he vanished with the faintest *pop*, like a bubble bursting.

Colin lay back, his mind whirling. He felt worn-out, as if he had been climbing many high mountains. As he lay there, thinking about all the weird things he had seen, his eyes slowly closed . . .

The next moment, or so it seemed, his mother was shaking him. "Come along, sleepyhead — breakfast's ready!"

He sat up, startled, staring around. The sun was shining in through the tent-flap, and everything seemed just as it should. His parents were packing up their things while breakfast simmered on the camp-stove just outside. It was all perfectly normal — like every other morning of their holiday.

Colin smiled. So it *had* been a dream. Even if it was a strange one — still vivid in his mind, not fading like dreams usually did.

Then he slid out of his sleeping bag — and his mother's eyes went wide.

"Colin, your pyjama legs! They're all *muddy* at the bottom! And *look* at your feet! Were you up, in the night, wandering outside?"

Colin stared down at his muddy legs and feet, feeling a jolt of cold fear deep in his stomach. "I . . . I think I was," he said.

"You must have had a nightmare," his mother said, "from all those scary stories of your father's, upsetting you. Never mind — have a wash, and put it out of your thoughts."

Colin nodded and began to pull off his pyjama top. But then he paused. There was something in the pyjama pocket — something pink and slimy, squashy and smelly. Goblin food.

Slowly he went to the door of the tent. His parents, busy with their packing, were not looking at him. Carefully he took out the mucky pink glob, and tossed it into the

bushes. Then he wiped his hand on his pyjama top — and tried to stop feeling cold and weak inside.

If the goblin food was real — then the party had been real. Not a dream. Every single horrible event that he remembered, from the night, had *really happened*.

But then he remembered the last thing Rankle had said to him. That he had nothing to fear any more — that none of the magical monsters could ever touch him again.

Taking a deep breath, Colin began to relax, even smiling a small wobbly smile. He had had a terrific adventure, he wasn't hurt in any way, and now he was safe, with nothing to fear.

Still smiling, he turned to his parents. "I don't think it was dad's stories that got me up last night," he said. "The stories don't upset me — I like them. And today I'm going to tell *you* a story — all about goblins and witches and things . . ."

First published in Great Britain 1988 by Victor Gollancz Ltd
14 Henrietta Street, London WC2E 8QJ



*British Library Cataloguing in Publication Data*
Hill, Douglas, *1935–*
Goblin party.
I. Title II. Demeyer, Paul
813′.54[J]

ISBN 0-575-04338-5

Printed in Singapore by Imago Publishing Ltd